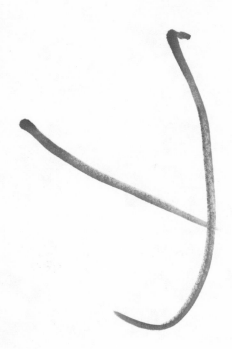

The Bee Sneeze

The
Bee Sneeze

by Beverly Keller
pictures by Diane Paterson

Coward, McCann & Geoghegan, Inc.
New York

To Anthony and Garrett

Text copyright © 1982 by Beverly Keller
Illustrations copyright © 1982 by Diane Paterson
Published simultaneously
in Canada by General Publishing Co. Limited, Toronto.
Printed in the United States of America
First printing
Library of Congress Cataloging in Publication Data
Keller, Beverly.
The bee sneeze.
Summary: Fiona rescues a bee from drowning
in her lemonade one hot summer day.
[1. Bees—Fiction. 2. Summer—Fiction]
I. Paterson, Diane, date. ill. II. Title.
PZ7.K2813Bd [E] 81-19509
ISBN 0-698-30740-2 AACR2

On a hot, hot summer Saturday,
Fiona Foster sat on her front porch.
Almost everyone she knew
had gone to the mountains
or the beach.

Fiona and her parents stayed home
because they didn't have a car.

Most people who had to stay in town
shut all their curtains
and sat in dark houses,
feeling cross and sticky.

Wearing old faded bathing suits,
Fiona's parents sat
barefoot in their living room
in front of an electric fan.

Fiona's friend Howard
came over with his dog Spike
and slumped on Fiona's porch steps.

"My folks want to go to the beach,"
Howard said,
"but Spike gets carsick."

"I do too," Fiona said.

"You want to go to the beach?"
Howard asked.

"I get carsick.
I know how Spike feels.
You should leave him here."

"Don't you want to come to the beach?"

"If I came,
you couldn't leave Spike here,"
Fiona pointed out.
"That means he'd come
to the beach, right?"

"You don't expect me
to leave my dog home *alone*
on a day like this?"

"No," Fiona said.
"It's just that I'm nervous
about riding with a carsick dog,
especially Spike.
Whenever I get in your car,
he sits on me.
Besides, I've got work to do here.
In hot weather,
bees drop in.
They drop in everywhere—
wading pools, birdbaths, water fountains.
Once they drop in,
they can't just drop out.
There'll be a lot of bees
to be saved today."

"Don't you ever wish
you saved something easy,
like string, or baseball cards?"
Howard asked.

Fiona nodded.
"It's scary work, saving bees,
but somebody has to do it.

Let me ask my parents
if Spike can stay here."

Fiona's parents
had put a dishpan full of ice
in front of the fan,
but they still felt miserable.

"May Howard leave Spike here
for the day?" Fiona asked.
"I don't want to ride to the beach
with a big, heavy, hairy, carsick dog
sitting on me and drooling."

Though her parents found this
a little confusing,
they were too hot to argue.

"He can stay on the porch
if you keep him quiet,
but he can't come in,"
Mrs. Foster said.

Fiona went out and told Spike, "Okay."

Howard hugged him
and promised to bring him
some driftwood, and told him
to stay with Fiona.

As soon as Howard was gone,
Spike began to howl.
When Fiona tried to hush him,
he barked.
Quickly, Fiona filled her dog dish
from the hose.

She kept the dish on her porch,
even though she had no pets,
in the hope some dog
might drop by for a drink.
Instead, bees dropped in.
Now she only filled the dish
when she was home
to fish out any bee who dropped in.

She put the full dog dish
in front of Spike.
"Have a drink."
She figured he couldn't
drink and bark at the same time.

He shivered and rolled his eyes
as if she were trying to poison him,
and he cried
shrill sharp dog cries.

Thinking he might not like
to drink alone,
Fiona went to the kitchen
and got a wheat roll for him
and a lemonade for herself.

"Keep that dog *quiet.*"
her father growled
as she went back to the front porch.

Fiona put the roll
in front of Spike.
"Here you go."

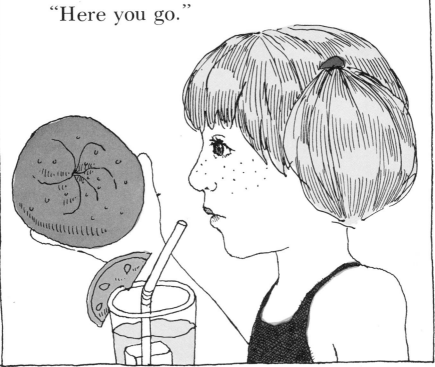

He nosed it off the porch,
then rolled on his back
with his legs stiff in the air,
looking like a large dead bug.

Fiona sat on the porch steps
wondering how
she was going to save bees
and take care of a dog
who wanted to be a large dead bug.
She couldn't help thinking
how cool and calm and simple
life would be
at the mountains or the beach.

While she wondered
if she should turn Spike over
before he got stuck that way,
a bee dropped in—
right into her lemonade.
He landed on an ice cube,
which turned over on top of him
at once.

17

"Oh, boy."
Setting down the glass,
Fiona ran down to the lawn
and found a dead leaf.
Then came the scary part.
The ice cube had turned over again,
with the bee on top of it.

Fiona managed to flick him off the cube
and fish him out with a leaf
before he was lost in a sea of ice.

In an ordinary bee rescue,
Fiona would simply put the leaf
and the bee in a sunny spot,
knowing that when he got dry,
he would be able to take care of himself.
She was not sure about this bee.
There were specks of lemon
all over him,
and there was a big lemon seed on his back.

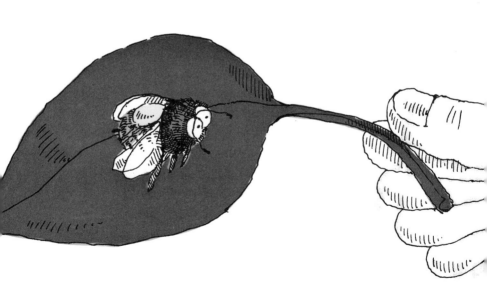

She wondered if the sugar
in the lemonade
had made him all sticky.
If he dried sticky, could he fly?
How do you unstick
a sticky bee?

Fiona was so worried,
she did one of the dumbest things
she had ever done.
Holding the leaf in her right hand,
she opened the front door with her left.

"How do you unstick . . ."

The air from the electric fan
blew the bee off the leaf
and whirled him, hurled him,
tossed him back out to the porch.

Fiona let the door slam shut
as her father said,
"Don't slam the door!"

On hands and knees
she searched the porch.
The bee was lying
like a small fuzzy lump
on the porch floor.

"Oh, bee!"
Fiona wondered
if his poor bee bones
were bruised.

Mr. Foster looked out the window.
"Our daughter
is on her hands and knees
talking to the porch floor,"
he said.

Dazed by the heat,
chilled by the lemonade,
blasted by the fan,
the bee sneezed.

A bee sneeze
is almost impossible
to see or hear or feel.
Not one person in a million
has ever noticed a bee sneeze.
However,
Fiona was nose to nose with that bee,
and paying close attention.
She saw him sneeze.

A butterfly,
faint from the heat of the day,
landed near Spike's ear.
She felt the bee sneeze
rush by her feelers.

Fiona ran into the living room.

"What's good for a bee sneeze?"
she gasped.

"I'm not even sure bees *have* knees,"
her mother said.

"Sneeze! Sneeze!" Fiona cried.
"What I do when I have a cold."

"I *thought* she was acting strange."
Mr. Foster hurried to get the thermometer.

Mrs. Foster felt Fiona's forehead.
"All you can do for a cold, dear,
is stay in bed, keep warm,
and drink a lot of juice."

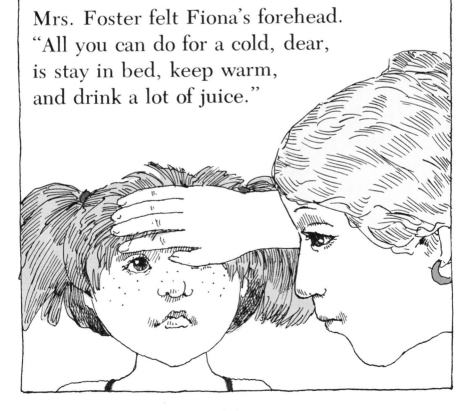

Mr. Foster put the thermometer
in Fiona's mouth.

She tried to show them.
in sign language
that there was an emergency outside
and she was needed on the porch.

"It's too hot to play charades, Fiona,"
her mother said.
"Especially if you have a cold."

Mr. Foster took the thermometer
and looked at it. "No fever."

Fiona hurried outside
before she got sent to bed.

Spike was sleeping,
looking like an upside-down,
hairy table.
The butterfly rested beside him.
On the porch floor
the bee still lay still.

Fiona looked around
for something that would make
a good bee bed.
How do you get a bee
to stay in bed?
Keeping him warm was easy
on a day like this,
but giving him a drink
would be a problem.
Suppose he needed somebody
to hold his head up?

The bee sneezed again.

This sneeze stirred the down
on the butterfly's wings.
It cooled her so that she
fluttered her wings.
They barely brushed
the tip of Spike's ear,
but the breeze they made
woke him and made him feel cooler
than he had felt all day.
He got up and took a drink,
remembering there was something
he was supposed to feel sad about,
but not able to remember what it was.

29

Since he had nothing better to do,
he plopped a heavy, hairy paw
on the edge of the dish.
The dish tipped,
something he always found interesting,
and water sloshed over the porch.

"Don't soak my bee!" Fiona cried
—too late.

"What is Fiona yelling?"
her father demanded.

"Something about
'Don't soap my tea,' "
Mrs. Foster said.

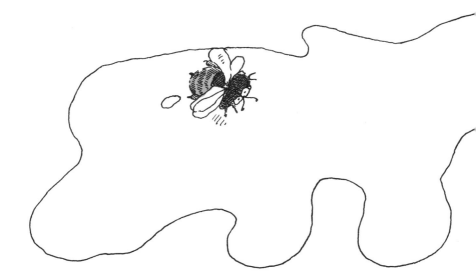

The water from the dog dish
flooded over the bee,
washing the lemonade and sugar
and even the seed off him.

Spike sat in the spilled water.
It felt wonderful, cool, and sloppy.
He wagged his tail.

"Don't wag the bee!" Fiona yelled
—too late.

"What *is* she screaming now?"
Mr. Foster groaned.

"She told someone
not to nag the sea,"
Mrs. Foster said.

Spike's tail swished the bee
right out of the water.

Too confused to sting,
the soggy, groggy bee
clung to the dog tail
for a terrible, wild ride.
He was waved up and down,
round and round,
and nearly out of his small bee mind.

"No! Halt! Stop!"
Fiona tried to catch Spike's tail
and rescue the bee.

Her father stormed out on the porch.
"Fiona Foster,
stop chasing that dog's tail!"

By now
Spike had shaken the bee quite dry.
Seeing Mr. Foster,
and Mrs. Foster, who came running out, too,
Spike wagged faster,
sending the bee spinning off his tail
and whirling off the porch.

Desperate and tailsick,
the bee quivered his wings.

Somehow, wobbly and dizzy,
he managed to fly away
fast, if not straight.

"Don't you ever let me see you
tease a dog again!"
Fiona's mother was furious.

Fiona's feelings were hurt.
"He had a bee on his tail."

"Oh. Well."
Her mother looked embarrassed.
"In that case, it was good of you
to save the dog from the bee."

Sitting in the water,
Spike offered to shake hands
with Mrs. Foster,
while his busy, soggy tail
whipped through the air.

"What I was doing . . ." Fiona began.

"You know, it's not so hot
out here now."

Sitting on the porch swing,
Mrs. Foster patted Spike,
which made him wag harder.
"Can you feel that breeze?
I don't know where it's coming from,
but it's wonderful."
With a push of her foot,
she started the swing moving.
Spike wagged faster.

"There is definitely a breeze
coming from somewhere.
I can feel it."
Mr. Foster climbed on the swing,
and Fiona joined him.

Mrs. Clancy, across the street,
looked through the curtains
of her stuffy, scorching living room.
"I think the Fosters
have all gone crazy!
They're out on the porch
in this blistering heat,
swinging on their porch swing like mad."

She came across the street
to see just how crazy they might be.
In front of their porch,
she stopped, amazed.
"Where is that breeze coming from?"

"Here. Come on up,"
Fiona's mother said.

"Hey, Clancy!" Mrs. Clancy called
to her husband across the street.
"Come on over. It's cooler here!"

Mr. Clancy came across the street,
bringing a carton of strawberry ice.

Fiona's father brought out
a pitcher of lemonade.

40

"If you have some old paper,"
Mrs. Clancy told Fiona,
"I'll show you
how to make fancy fans."

Mr. Stein, next door,
came out to look for his mail.

Fiona's mother waved to him.
"Come on over! We've got a breeze here."

Mr. Stein brought over a pound cake.

A few more people
who couldn't get to the beach
or the mountains
heard the talking and laughing
on Fiona's porch.

They looked out,
wondering who had gone crazy
from the heat.
"Come on over!" Mr. Foster told them.
"I think we're having a party."

They all came,
with potato salad and cole slaw,
pickles and chips,
melons and blueberries.

They petted Spike
and gave him treats
and told him what a great,
handsome dog he was.

Spike wagged
as he had never wagged before.

"What's going on?
Did somebody have an accident?"
Back from the beach,
with a sunburned nose
and sand in his hair,
Howard ran up the porch steps.
Spike danced and yelped
and licked his face.

"It's a great party!" Fiona told him.
She found Howard a plate
and helped him fill it.
Spike helped him empty it.

Sitting on the swing,
Howard hugged his dog,
whose tail moved
like a furry windshield wiper.
"I don't know whether
it's because of the breeze,
or the cold food and drinks,
or because everybody's having
such a good time,
but the heat doesn't bother me
here on your porch."

Drawn by melon and lemonade,
the butterfly fluttered by.
Buzzing back
to taste this and that,
the bee dropped into the berry juice
on Howard's plate.

"Get out of here, bee!"
Howard yelled.

46

The bee flew away,
feeling his fuzzy feet
pleasantly sticky.
Nobody watched him go.
Nobody wished him well.
Nobody realized his sneeze
had started the whole party,
but then,
bees don't expect much from people.

About the Author

Beverly Keller was born in San Francisco and attended schools in Colorado, South Dakota, Nebraska, Washington, D. C., and California. A period spent living in the Middle East inspired her to write an espionage novel, *The Baghdad Defections*. Since then she has written six well-received children's books: *Fiona's Flea*, *Fiona's Bee*, *Don't Throw Another One, Dover!*, *The Beetle Bush*, and *Pimm's Place*, all picture books; and for older readers: *The Genuine, Ingenious Thrift Shop Genie, Clarissa Mae Bean & Me*.

Ms. Keller makes her home in Davis, California.

About the Artist

Diane Paterson lives in High Falls, N.Y., with her two daughters, two cats, a chicken and a rooster, and a dozen turkeys. She has written and illustrated about twenty books so far, including *Fiona's Flea*, and is now working on a giant story book for children.